A Week in a Mortal Skin

Viola Giselle

Dedication Page

This book is dedicated to the Celestia who dreamt of stars, and the one who carries the echo of human hearts:

This story, a celestial tapestry woven with threads of memory, love, and loss, is a gift for you. It's a reflection held up to the vastness of time, capturing the spark that ignited your journey and the profound transformation you embraced.

To the younger you, filled with wonder and the promise of a future yet unwritten, this is a reminder. Never lose sight of the celestial fire that burns within. Embrace the audacious dreams that propel you forward, and remember, even the faintest star can illuminate the darkest night.

And to the future you, gazing upon the celestial expanse with a heart touched by humanity, this is a testament. May you never forget the warmth of human connection, the bittersweet beauty of fleeting moments, and the love that transcends even the boundaries of existence.

This story is a bridge, a shimmering filament woven from the tapestry of your experiences. May it serve as a guiding light, reminding you that you are a being of both celestial wonder and profound human empathy

Chapter 1
Descent of Dreams

In the heart of the celestial palace, where golden arches stretched towards the heavens and ethereal light danced upon marble floors, I found myself seated beside my dear friend, Seraphiel, within the hallowed chamber of the celestial council. "Okay, Celestia, spill it," Seraphiel, his radiant wings shimmering with celestial light, nudged me playfully. "What's with the determined look?"

With a soft chuckle, I turned to face him, the weight of my decision heavy upon my ethereal form. "I've got this crazy idea, Seraphiel," I confessed, my voice echoing softly against the chamber's grandeur. "I want to experience life on Earth firsthand. You know, walk among mortals, feel what they feel, all that jazz." Seraphiel's eyes widened in surprise, then lit up with understanding. "Whoa, that's bold, Celestia. But why now? You've been content up here for eons."

"I know, I know," I nodded eagerly, my silver eyes gleaming with determination. "But lately, I've been feeling this... longing. A curiosity to understand humanity on a deeper level. And I just can't shake it." He gave me a knowing smile, the celestial light casting intricate patterns upon the chamber's walls. "Well, you've certainly got the adventurous spirit for it. But you do realize the council doesn't hand out earthly vacations like candy, right?"

I chuckled nervously, nodding in agreement. "Yeah, I know it won't be easy. But I've got to try, Seraphiel. I feel it in my wings – this is something I need to do." As the celestial council deliberated my request, I exchanged a hopeful glance with Seraphiel, my heart pounding with anticipation. Would they grant my wish? Only time would tell.

As the celestial council deliberated my request, time seemed to stretch infinitely within the hallowed chamber. Each passing moment was laden with anticipation, my heart beating in rhythm with the celestial pulse that echoed throughout the palace.

Finally, after what felt like an eternity, the archangel Gabriel, resplendent in his luminous robes, rose from his seat at the head of the council chamber. His voice, commanding yet gentle, filled the space with an otherworldly resonance.

"Celestia," he spoke, his words carrying the weight of celestial authority, "your request has been heard, and your plea has touched the hearts of the celestial council."

A surge of hope and trepidation welled within me as I awaited his next words, my silver eyes fixed upon his radiant form. "It is decreed," Gabriel continued, his gaze unwavering, "that you shall be granted a single week to descend from the heavens and walk among mortals." Relief washed over me, mingled with a profound sense of gratitude towards the council for granting my wish. But as Gabriel spoke, I sensed a solemnity in his tone that gave me pause.

"But heed this warning, Celestia," Gabriel's voice resonated with solemnity, "your journey on Earth shall be governed by the laws of the celestial realm. You must abide by these rules, for they are immutable."

I listened intently as Gabriel proceeded to explain the rules that would govern my earthly sojourn. "In order to immerse yourself fully in the mortal experience," Gabriel began, "a veil shall be placed upon your mind. This memory block will shield you from the knowledge of your true celestial identity. You shall live as a mortal, with no recollection of your angelic nature."

As Gabriel continued, his words carried the weight of centuries of celestial wisdom.

"Your time on Earth shall be limited," he explained. "A span of seven days is all you shall have. At the end of this time, you shall return to the celestial realm, your memories of the mortal world fading like morning mist." Finally, Gabriel's tone grew somber as he spoke of the final rule. "Love, Celestia," he said, his voice tinged with sadness, "is a powerful force that transcends time and space. But you must not form romantic attachments with mortals. Such entanglements may disrupt the natural order of the celestial realm."

I nodded solemnly, understanding the gravity of his words and the magnitude of my request. Before I could voice my gratitude, Gabriel continued, addressing the reason for the council's decision. "Your request, Celestia," he said, his eyes softening with compassion, "was not taken lightly. But your unwavering dedication to understanding the human experience, coupled with your compassion for mortals, convinced the council of the sincerity of your intentions. May your journey bring enlightenment to both you and those you encounter." With each rule, the weight of my newfound responsibility settled upon my shoulders. I nodded solemnly, acknowledging the gravity of Gabriel's words and the challenges that lay ahead.

"And remember," Gabriel added, his gaze piercing, "the celestial council shall be watching over you, guiding your path and protecting you from harm. Trust in their wisdom, Celestia, and may your journey be filled with enlightenment and discovery."

With a final blessing from the celestial council, I rose from my seat, my heart brimming with excitement and anticipation for the adventure that awaited me.

As I prepared to embark on my journey to the mortal realm, Seraphiel approached me, his radiant wings aglow with celestial light.

"Are you ready for this, Celestia?" he asked, his voice filled with concern and support.

I smiled, my wings tingling with anticipation. "More than ready, Seraphiel. Let's make this week one to remember." With a nod of affirmation, Seraphiel extended his hand towards me, the celestial light of his touch suffusing my being with warmth and reassurance. But before we could proceed further, Seraphiel began to recite the rules once more, his voice tinged with a sense of duty.

"Celestia," he began, his tone solemn, "remember, your time on Earth shall be limited to a span of seven days. At the end of this time, you shall return to the celestial realm, your memories of the mortal world fading like morning mist."

I felt a surge of irritation rising within me at his repetition of the rules. Didn't he trust me to remember? "And remember," Seraphiel continued, unaware of my growing frustration, "you must not form romantic attachments with mortals. Love is a powerful force, Celestia, one that transcends time and space. But such entanglements may disrupt the natural order of the celestial realm."

His words grated against my patience, the weight of his caution feeling stifling.

"Seraphiel," I interrupted him, my voice laced with irritation, "I know the rules. You don't need to repeat them to me." He paused, taken aback by my sudden outburst, before offering an apologetic smile. "Forgive me, Celestia," he said, his voice gentle yet contrite. "I only wish to ensure your safety and the success of your mission."

I sighed, the tension within me easing slightly at his understanding.

"Thank you, Seraphiel," I replied, my irritation dissipating as quickly as it had arisen.

In that moment, I reached out to grasp Seraphiel's hand, the connection between us a tangible reminder of our shared journey. "Thank you, Seraphiel," I said, my voice soft with gratitude. "For always being there for me, through every trial and triumph."

His gaze met mine, a mirror of understanding and camaraderie. "It's been an honor, Celestia," he replied, his voice a gentle echo in the celestial chamber. "Watching you grow and thrive has been one of the greatest joys of my existence." I squeezed his hand gently, a silent promise etched in the depths of my celestial soul. "I will come back, Seraphiel," I whispered, determination lacing my words. "No matter what trials may come, I will return to the celestial realm."

Seraphiel's expression softened, a flicker of curiosity lighting his eyes. "And what is your plan, Celestia?" he inquired, his voice gentle yet probing. "How do you intend to navigate the complexities of the mortal world?" I smiled, a sense of purpose guiding my words. "I will immerse myself in the human experience," I replied, my voice filled with determination. "I will observe, learn, and above all, I will strive to understand what it means to be truly human."

Remember, the mortal realm can be both beautiful and dangerous. Proceed with caution, and never forget who you are." His words resonated within me, a solemn reminder of the challenges that lay ahead. "I will, Seraphiel," I promised, my voice steady with resolve. "And I will carry your guidance with me every step of the way."

As we stood there, a sense of heaviness settled over us. Seraphiel's desire to accompany me was palpable, his eyes betraying the longing within his celestial heart.

"I wish I could go with you, Celestia," he confessed, his voice tinged with regret. "To see you off and ensure your safety." I reached out and gently squeezed his hand, offering what comfort I could. "I know, Seraphiel," I said softly. "But the council's decree is clear. It's for the best that you remain here."

Seraphiel nodded, though the disappointment still lingered in his eyes. "I understand," he replied, resignation coloring his tone. "But know that my thoughts will be with you every moment you're away." With a final exchange of glances, Seraphiel and I shared a silent understanding. Though separated by realms, our bond remained unbreakable.

I turned to leave, a sudden impulse stirred within me. I reached out and enveloped Seraphiel in a warm embrace, the celestial light of our connection shining brightly.

"Until we meet again," I whispered, my voice carrying the weight of our shared history.

"Until we meet again," Seraphiel echoed, his embrace a comforting anchor in the sea of uncertainty. And with that, I stepped away, my heart heavy yet filled with determination. I made my way towards the portal leading to the mortal realm, a figure emerged from the celestial chamber. It was Gabriel, the revered Archangel known for his wisdom and strength.

"Celestia," he called out, his voice resonating with celestial authority.

I turned to face him, a sense of reverence washing over me. "Archangel Gabriel," I greeted with a respectful bow of my head. "To what do I owe the honor of your presence?" Gabriel approached with purpose, his celestial aura radiating with divine light. "I have come to speak with you before you embark on your mission," he declared, his voice commanding yet compassionate.

I nodded, eager to hear his words. "I am grateful for your guidance, Archangel," I replied, my voice filled with humility. He studied me for a moment, his gaze penetrating yet gentle. "Celestia, your curiosity about the mortal realm is commendable," he began, his voice carrying the weight of centuries of wisdom. "But remember, with knowledge comes responsibility. The mortal realm is a place of both wonder and peril." I listened intently, absorbing his words. "I understand, Archangel," I affirmed, a sense of determination rising within me. "I will tread carefully and approach each discovery with reverence."

Gabriel nodded, a hint of approval in his expression. "Good," he said, his voice softened by compassion. "May your journey be filled with enlightenment and understanding, Celestia. And may you always remember the light that guides you."

His words stirred something deep within me, a sense of purpose and resolve. "Thank you, Archangel Gabriel," I replied sincerely, gratitude filling my celestial heart. "Your words have strengthened my resolve, and I will carry them with me as I venture into the unknown."

With a final nod of affirmation, Gabriel stepped back, his presence a beacon of celestial authority. As I stood before the shimmering portal, I felt a surge of determination coursing through my celestial essence. With one last glance towards Gabriel, I offered him a silent vow—a promise to honor his guidance and approach each discovery with reverence and humility. And with that, I stepped through the portal, leaving behind the celestial realm and embarking on my journey into the unknown. The celestial realm faded from view, replaced by swirling vortexes of color and light. I descended from the heavens and into the embrace of the mortal world, I knew that my path would be fraught with challenges and trials. Yet, I was determined to face them. For I was Celestia, angelic emissary to the mortal realm, and my journey had only just begun.

Chapter 2
Arrival on Mortal Realm

I awoke to the gentle caress of sunlight filtering through a small window, its warm rays casting a golden hue over the room. The soft trill of birdsong filled the air, accompanied by the distant murmur of bustling activity. Slowly, I opened my eyes, blinking against the unfamiliar brightness. I found myself in a cozy bedroom, the walls adorned with delicate floral wallpaper. The room was modest yet inviting, with simple wooden furniture and a small dresser topped with a vase of fresh flowers. The quilted blanket covering me added a touch of warmth, and a subtle scent of lavender lingered in the air, calming my disoriented mind.

As I sat up, a wave of disorientation washed over me. Where was I? How did I get here? My mind was a foggy haze, filled with fragmented memories that slipped away the moment I tried to grasp them. I glanced around the room, searching for something—anything—that might anchor me to reality. My gaze landed on a mirror hanging on the wall opposite the bed. Hesitantly, I swung my legs over the side of the bed and stood, my movements tentative as I approached the mirror. When I caught sight of my reflection, I was taken aback.

The face staring back at me was unfamiliar, yet somehow it felt like my own. My features were those of a young woman with soft brown hair and wide, curious eyes. I raised a hand to touch my face, the sensation both strange and familiar. Before I could dwell further on my thoughts, a gentle knock sounded at the door. I turned, my heart racing with a mix of anticipation and uncertainty. The door creaked open, revealing a kindly woman with a warm smile and kind eyes that crinkled at the corners.

"Good morning, dear," she greeted, her voice soothing and melodic. "I'm Agnes. You must be hungry." I nodded slowly, still trying to piece together my thoughts. "Where am I?" I asked, my voice barely above a whisper.

Agnes stepped into the room, her presence radiating warmth and reassurance. "You're in my home, in the small town of Meadowbrook. You were found outside the bakery last night, looking lost and confused. I brought you here to rest." I felt a wave of gratitude wash over me. "Thank you, Agnes. I... I don't remember anything. Not even my name."

Agnes approached the bed and sat down beside me, her expression compassionate. "It's alright, dear. Sometimes the mind takes its time to recover. You're safe here. We'll figure things out together. For now, why don't we call you Clara?"

I nodded, feeling a sense of comfort in her presence. "Clara. Yes, that sounds right. Thank you, Agnes."

Agnes handed me a simple dress, soft to the touch, and guided me to a small bathroom adjacent to the bedroom. As I changed out of the nightgown and into the dress, I marveled at the sensation of the fabric against my skin. Every detail of this world felt vivid and real, yet there was a lingering sense of something missing.

Once I was dressed, Agnes led me to a small kitchen where the aroma of freshly baked bread and brewed coffee filled the air. The kitchen was quaint, with wooden cabinets and a checkered tablecloth covering a small dining table. The rich, comforting scents wrapped around me, making my stomach growl in anticipation.

"Here, have some breakfast," Agnes offered, placing a plate of toast, eggs, and fruit in front of me. "You must be hungry." I realized she was right; a gnawing hunger had settled in my stomach. I thanked her and began to eat, savoring each bite as if it were my first meal. The flavors were rich and comforting, grounding me in the present moment. As I ate, Agnes sat across from me, sipping her coffee and studying me with gentle curiosity. "Do you remember anything at all, Clara? Where you came from, or how you ended up here?"

I shook my head, frustration bubbling beneath the surface. "No, it's all a blank. I feel like I should remember, but I just... can't." Agnes reached across the table and squeezed my hand reassuringly. "Don't worry, dear. Memories have a way of returning when the time is right. For now, just focus on settling in and getting to know the town."

I nodded, grateful for her kindness. "Thank you, Agnes. I'll do my best." After breakfast, Agnes suggested a walk around Meadowbrook. I agreed, grateful for her guidance. The morning air was crisp and fresh as we stepped outside, and I inhaled deeply, savoring the scents of grass and flowers. Meadowbrook was a quaint town with charming cottages and blooming gardens. As we walked, I admired the beauty around me, feeling a sense of peace.

Our first stop was Agnes's bakery, a cozy little shop with a sign that read "Agnes's Bakes." The aroma of freshly baked bread and pastries wafted out, mingling with the scent of brewing coffee. Agnes unlocked the door and ushered me inside. "This is where I spend most of my days," she said with a smile. "Feel free to look around."

The bakery was warm and inviting, with shelves lined with all kinds of baked goods. I could hear the faint hum of an oven in the back, and the air was filled with the comforting smell of dough and sugar. As I explored, Agnes introduced me to a few regular customers who had stopped by for their morning treats. "Everyone, this is Clara," she announced. "She's new in town and staying with me for a while."

A chorus of greetings met me. A woman with an apron dusted with flour stepped forward. "Welcome, Clara! I'm Martha, and I help out here sometimes. If you ever need anything, just ask." "Thank you, Martha," I replied, shaking her hand. "It's nice to meet you all." Agnes busied herself behind the counter, preparing orders and restocking the shelves. I wanted to help, to do something useful, but I wasn't sure where to start. I watched her move with practiced efficiency, feeling a sense of admiration for her skill.

"Is there anything I can do to help?" I asked tentatively.

Agnes glanced over, a warm smile on her face. "Oh, that's very kind of you, Clara. How about you help me with these muffins?" She handed me a tray of muffin batter and pointed to a row of empty tins. "Just scoop the batter into the tins, like this," she demonstrated, "and then pop them in the oven." I nodded, eager to lend a hand. But as I attempted to scoop the batter, my hand slipped, and I ended up knocking over a container of flour. White powder exploded into the air, coating everything in a fine dust.

"Oh, dear!" I exclaimed, flustered and apologetic. "I'm so sorry, Agnes. I didn't mean to..."

Agnes chuckled softly, coming to my rescue once again. "It's alright, Clara. Accidents happen." She grabbed a cloth and began wiping down the counter, her smile reassuring.

I hurriedly helped clean up the mess, cheeks burning with embarrassment. Despite my best intentions, it seemed I was more of a hindrance than a help in the bakery.

As the day wore on, I continued to assist Agnes in small ways, trying my best to avoid any further mishaps. Though my contributions were clumsy, Agnes never once made me feel inadequate. Instead, she encouraged me to keep trying, reminding me that mistakes were a natural part of learning.

As I watched the customers come and go, their faces lighting up with delight as they sampled Agnes's creations, I couldn't help but feel a sense of confusion. How could something as simple as baked goods bring people so much joy? It was a concept that eluded me, yet I found myself drawn to the warmth and camaraderie of the bakery, despite my lack of understanding.

After helping Agnes close up the bakery for the day, we stepped outside into the late afternoon sun. The sky was a brilliant shade of blue, with fluffy white clouds drifting lazily overhead.

"Would you like to take a stroll around town, Clara?" Agnes suggested, her eyes twinkling with excitement. I smiled, eager to explore more of Meadowbrook. "That sounds wonderful, Agnes." We wandered through the streets of Meadowbrook, soaking in the sights and sounds of the bustling town. Children played in the park, their laughter echoing in the air, while couples strolled hand in hand, enjoying the warmth of the sun.

As we walked, Agnes pointed out various landmarks, sharing stories and anecdotes about the town and its residents. I listened intently, absorbing every detail, eager to learn more about my new home. Along the way, I couldn't help but notice that my tone had become a bit curt and impatient, unintentionally overshadowing Agnes's cheerful chatter. "Clara, is everything alright?" Agnes asked gently, her eyes searching mine.

I hesitated, realizing that my abruptness may have come across as rude. "I'm sorry, Agnes," I said, feeling a pang of guilt. "I didn't mean to sound... dismissive. It's just... I'm still trying to adjust to everything, and I guess I'm feeling a bit overwhelmed."

Agnes nodded understandingly, her warm smile returning. "It's okay, dear. I can only imagine how strange this must all feel for you. Just know that I'm here for you, whenever you need someone to talk to."

I felt a wave of gratitude wash over me, touched by Agnes's kindness and understanding. "Thank you, Agnes. That means a lot to me." As we resumed our stroll, I made a conscious effort to be more mindful of my words and tone, striving to be more patient and considerate in my interactions with Agnes and the townsfolk.

But despite my efforts, I couldn't shake the feeling that others in the town viewed me as rude and aloof. I caught snippets of whispered conversations as we passed by, and I could sense the judgmental glances directed my way. "Did you hear how Clara spoke to Agnes?"

"I know, right? She seemed so dismissive and ungrateful."

"I don't think she'll ever fit in here."

The words stung, and I felt a knot form in my stomach. I wanted nothing more than to prove them wrong, to show them that I was capable of kindness and warmth.

"Clara," Agnes began gently, "remember, Meadowbrook is a place where kindness and understanding go a long way. People here appreciate sincerity and warmth. Just be yourself, and you'll fit right in."

I nodded, taking her words to heart. "I'll try my best, Agnes."

With Agnes by my side, offering guidance and support, I felt reassured as we continued our walk through the charming streets of Meadowbrook. Despite the challenges of adjusting to my new life, I was determined to do my best to fit in and make Meadowbrook my home.

As the sun began its descent, painting the sky with hues of pink and gold, Agnes and I walked through Meadowbrook, our footsteps echoing softly against the cobblestone streets. The town seemed to glow with a warm, inviting light, and I couldn't help but feel a sense of peace settle over me. Agnes glanced at me, her eyes sparkling with excitement. "Clara, I have a little surprise for you," she said, her voice filled with anticipation.

My heart skipped a beat at her words, a rush of exhilaration coursing through me. Why was I feeling this way? It was as if a veil had been lifted, revealing a whole new world of possibilities. For the first time since arriving in Meadowbrook, I felt a flicker of excitement, a glimmer of hope that perhaps, just perhaps, my life here could be filled with joy and adventure.

"A surprise?" I echoed, unable to conceal the wonder in my voice. "What is it?" My eyes widened with curiosity, eager to uncover the mystery that lay ahead.

Agnes grinned mischievously, her eyes twinkling with delight. "Tomorrow, we're going on a special outing together," she revealed. "I think you'll really enjoy it."

The anticipation swelled within me, a sense of exhilaration building with each passing moment. Why was this so thrilling? It was a feeling I had never experienced before, a sense of wonder and excitement that filled me with a newfound sense of hope.

"An outing? That sounds wonderful, Agnes. Thank you," I breathed, a smile spreading across my face as I imagined the adventures that awaited us. As we continued our stroll through the enchanting streets of Meadowbrook, I couldn't help but question myself. Why was I feeling this way? What was it about this surprise that had ignited such a spark within me?

Chapter 3
Experiencing Humanity 2.0

As I awoke to the gentle rays of the morning sun streaming through the curtains, a sense of eager anticipation filled my heart. Today was the day of Agnes's surprise outing, and I couldn't wait to see what adventures awaited me. With a quick glance around my modest room, I realized I had no other clothes than the ones I wore the day before. A pang of disappointment briefly tugged at my excitement. Nevertheless, I resolved to make the best of it. After all, it wasn't about the clothes but the experiences that awaited me.

I hastily smoothed down the fabric of my blouse and adjusted my jeans, hoping they looked presentable enough for whatever the day had in store. As I slipped on my worn sneakers. Agnes's cheerful voice echoed from downstairs. "Clara, are you ready for our adventure?" she called out, her excitement palpable even from afar.

With a smile, I made my way downstairs to find Agnes waiting for me, a bright grin on her face. "Good morning, Agnes," I greeted her warmly. "I'm as ready as I'll ever be."

Agnes's eyes twinkled with mischief as she eyed my outfit. "You know what, Clara? I think it's time you had something new," she said, her voice filled with determination.

I blinked in surprise, not expecting her suggestion. "But Agnes, I don't have any other clothes," I replied, a hint of uncertainty creeping into my voice.

Agnes waved off my concerns with a dismissive flick of her hand. "Nonsense! We'll just have to remedy that, won't we?" she exclaimed, her enthusiasm contagious.

Before I could protest further, Agnes disappeared into her bedroom and returned moments later with a flowy blouse and a pair of jeans. "Here, you can borrow these," she said, handing me the clothes with a smile. I hesitated for a moment, touched by her gesture. "Are you sure, Agnes? I wouldn't want to impose," I said, feeling a surge of gratitude for her kindness.

Agnes waved away my concerns with a laugh. "Nonsense, Clara! Consider it a loan from one friend to another. Now let's get you dressed and ready for our adventure!"

With a grateful smile, I accepted Agnes's offer and quickly changed into the borrowed clothes. As I looked at myself in the mirror, I couldn't help but feel a sense of excitement building within me.

As I descended the staircase, the anticipation bubbled within me like a fizzy drink ready to overflow. Each step felt lighter, as if I were already floating on the excitement of what awaited me downstairs. there stood Agnes, her eyes gleaming with an excitement that matched my own. "Good morning, Clara!" Agnes greeted me, her smile infectious. "Are you ready for our adventure?"

My heart leaped with anticipation. "Absolutely! I've been waiting for this," I replied, barely able to contain my excitement. Agnes's eyes sparkled with mischief as she leaned in closer. "Today, we're going to a special charity event in town," she revealed in a conspiratorial tone. "It's a chance for us to give back to the community and make a difference together."

A rush of warmth flooded through me at Agnes's words. "That sounds incredible, Agnes. I'm so grateful to be a part of it," I exclaimed, a wide grin spreading across my face. With a shared sense of excitement, Agnes and I exchanged knowing glances before heading out the door together. Agnes and I strolled towards the charity event, the warm rays of the sun casting golden hues around us, I couldn't shake the question that had been weighing on my mind.

"Agnes," I started tentatively, glancing sideways at her, "I can't help but wonder... why are you being so kind to me? You barely know me."

Agnes's steps faltered momentarily, her gaze meeting mine with a mixture of surprise and understanding. "Clara," she began, her voice soft yet resolute, "I believe in the power of kindness. And besides," she added with a small smile, "there's something about you that just feels... special." Her words caught me off guard, stirring a mix of emotions within me. "Special? Me?" I echoed, incredulous.

Agnes nodded, her smile widening. "Yes, you," she affirmed. "There's a light in you, Clara, a warmth and compassion that's rare to find. It's like you have this innate ability to brighten up even the darkest of days." I couldn't help but feel a lump form in my throat at Agnes's heartfelt words. "Thank you, Agnes," I murmured, touched by her kindness. "But why me? Why now?" Agnes's expression softened, her eyes reflecting a depth of emotion that took my breath away. "Because, Clara," she replied, her voice barely above a whisper, "life is short, and we never know how much time we have left. I want to spend whatever time I have making a difference, spreading love and kindness wherever I go. And in you, I see a kindred spirit, someone who shares that same desire to make the world a better place."

Tears welled up in my eyes as Agnes's words washed over me, filling me with a sense of purpose and belonging I hadn't felt in a long time. "Thank you, Agnes," I repeated, my voice choked with emotion. "I'm so grateful to have you in my life."

With a shared understanding and a renewed sense of purpose, Agnes and I continued our journey towards the charity event, our hearts connected by the unbreakable bonds of friendship and love. And as we walked, I knew that whatever the future held, I would always cherish the memories of this shared journey with Agnes by my side.

I entered the bustling venue of the charity event, Agnes and I were immediately greeted by the vibrant energy of the community.

"Wow, look at all this," I remarked, my eyes wide with wonder as I took in the scene before us. Agnes beamed at my reaction, her hand resting reassuringly on my shoulder. "Isn't it amazing?" she replied, her voice filled with pride. "Everyone has come together to make a difference today."

I nodded, feeling a swell of emotion in my chest as I watched volunteers bustling about, serving meals and offering assistance to those in need.

"It's truly inspiring," I murmured, my voice barely above a whisper.

Agnes squeezed my shoulder gently, a knowing smile playing on her lips. "That's the power of community," she said. "When we come together with a common purpose, there's nothing we can't achieve."

As we made our way through the crowd, I couldn't help but notice the banners and posters adorning the walls, each one highlighting a different aspect of the charity's mission. From providing meals to the homeless to supporting local schools and community centers, it was clear that this event was about more than just charity—it was about building a stronger, more compassionate community for everyone.

With a shared sense of purpose, Agnes and I joined the ranks of volunteers, eager to lend our own hands to the cause. As we served meals and offered assistance to those in need, I felt a profound sense of fulfillment wash over me. Here, surrounded by kindness and compassion as I looked around at the faces of my fellow volunteers, I felt grateful to be a part of such a caring and compassionate community.

During the event, amidst the vibrant tapestry of bustling activity and heartwarming displays of community spirit, I found myself unexpectedly drawn into a chance encounter with a stranger. "Excuse me," a warm voice interrupted my thoughts, and I turned to see a friendly face beside me, a gentle smile playing on his lips. His tousled chestnut hair framed a face that radiated kindness, and his eyes sparkled with genuine warmth as they met mine.

"I couldn't help but notice your kindness earlier when you helped that elderly lady. It's truly inspiring," he remarked, his tone sincere and genuine. Surprised by his observation, I returned his smile, but in my haste, I accidentally knocked over a stack of pamphlets. They scattered across the ground, causing a few nearby attendees to glance in our direction. "Oh, I'm so sorry," I exclaimed, quickly bending down to gather the fallen pamphlets. "I didn't mean to..."

The stranger knelt down beside me, his movements graceful and fluid. With a reassuring chuckle, he began to help me gather the scattered papers. "No worries," he said, his voice calm and soothing. "Looks like we're both a bit clumsy, huh?"

I couldn't help but laugh at the irony of the situation. "Seems that way," I replied, feeling a sense of camaraderie building between us.

As we continued to gather the pamphlets, I stole a quick glance at the stranger beside me. His easygoing demeanor and genuine smile put me at ease, and I found myself drawn to his warmth and sincerity. With the pamphlets gathered and returned to their rightful place, I finally had the chance to properly meet the stranger. "I'm Daniel, by the way," he introduced himself with a friendly smile.

I shook his hand, struck by the genuine warmth in his touch. "Nice to meet you, Daniel. I'm Clara." As our conversation continued, I couldn't help but feel a growing sense of connection to Daniel. There was something about him that felt familiar, as if we were meant to meet in this moment. And as we bid each other farewell and went our separate ways, I couldn't help but feel grateful for the unexpected encounter and the newfound connection it had brought into my life.

In the fading light of dusk, my footsteps echoed softly against the cobblestone streets of Meadowbrook. The day's events danced through my mind like flickering candle flames, each memory igniting a warm ember of gratitude within my heart.

Beside me, Agnes walked in companionable silence, her presence a comforting anchor in the gentle twilight. I stole a glance at my friend, feeling a swell of appreciation for the kindness and warmth she had shown me throughout the day.

"It's been quite a day, hasn't it?" I ventured, breaking the peaceful quiet that enveloped us.

Agnes smiled, her eyes reflecting the soft hues of the setting sun. "Indeed it has," she replied, her voice soft and gentle. "But it's moments like these that remind me of the beauty and goodness in the world." I nodded in agreement, my heart echoing Agnes's sentiment. In the tranquil embrace of dusk, I found myself reflecting on the unexpected connections I had made, from the bustling charity event to my brief encounter with Daniel.

As we continued our journey homeward, I felt a deep sense of contentment settle over me like a comforting blanket. True happiness, I realized, lay not in grand adventures or material possessions, but in the simple moments of connection shared with others.

And as the last rays of sunlight melted into the horizon, I knew that I was exactly where I was meant to be, surrounded by the warmth of friendship and the gentle embrace of community. In the quiet beauty of dusk, I found solace and peace, grateful for the journey that had led me here.

Chapter 4
Tides of Emotion

In the days that followed my arrival in Meadowbrook, I found myself navigating the unpredictable currents of human emotion with a mixture of trepidation and curiosity. Each passing moment seemed to bring with it a new wave of feelings, from the exhilarating highs of joy and laughter to the crushing lows of heartache and uncertainty. One moment found me immersed in the pure joy of friendship, the kind that feels like coming home after a long journey. Agnes's presence enveloped me like a warm embrace, her unwavering support and companionship grounding me in the present moment.

"Can you believe we stumbled upon this little café?" Agnes exclaimed, her eyes alight with excitement as we stepped into a cozy corner establishment.

I chuckled, the aroma of freshly brewed coffee mingling with the scent of freshly baked pastries. "It's like something out of a storybook," I replied, feeling a sense of wonder wash over me. Together, we embarked on adventures through the enchanting streets of Meadowbrook, each corner revealing a new delight waiting to be discovered. From quaint cafes serving steaming mugs of aromatic coffee to bustling markets teeming with vibrant colors and lively chatter, we drank in the sights and sounds of our surroundings with wide-eyed wonder.

As we wandered through the bustling market square, Agnes turned to me with a grin. "I never get tired of exploring this town with you, Clara," she said, her voice tinged with affection. I smiled back, feeling a warmth spread through my chest. "Me neither, Agnes. It's like every corner holds a new adventure."

Our laughter echoed through the cobblestone streets like music, a symphony of joy and camaraderie that resonated with the pulse of the town. In Agnes's company, every moment felt infused with a sense of magic, as if the world itself was conspiring to bring us closer together. In her presence, I felt a sense of belonging I had never known before, a deep-rooted connection that transcended the barriers of time and space. We shared stories and dreams beneath the soft glow of street lamps, our voices blending harmoniously in the quiet of the night.

"I'm grateful for you, Agnes," I confessed, the words spilling from my lips without hesitation. Agnes reached out and squeezed my hand, her smile radiant in the dim light. "And I'm grateful for you, Clara. You've brought so much joy into my life." Our bond was forged in moments of shared laughter and quiet understanding, each memory etched into the fabric of our friendship like a precious gem. Together, we weathered the storms of life and celebrated its joys, united in our shared journey through the winding paths of fate.

Yet amidst the joyous moments of camaraderie and laughter, I found myself grappling with the unfamiliar sensation of love's sweet sting. It was a feeling that took me by surprise, creeping into my heart like a thief in the night and leaving me breathless in its wake. "Clara, you seem distracted today," Agnes observed, her brow furrowing with concern as we sat together in the cozy corner of the café.

I offered her a faint smile, trying to mask the whirlwind of emotions churning within me. "I suppose I have a lot on my mind," I admitted, my gaze drifting to the window where the sunlight danced upon the cobblestone streets. Agnes reached out and gently squeezed my hand, her touch a comforting anchor in the storm of my thoughts. "You know you can talk to me about anything, right?" I nodded, grateful for her understanding and support. "I know, Agnes. It's just... there's someone I can't seem to get out of my mind."

Her eyes widened with curiosity, a knowing smile playing at the corners of her lips. "A special someone, perhaps?" I felt a blush rise to my cheeks, the truth of her words hanging in the air between us like a delicate veil. "Maybe," I confessed, my voice barely above a whisper.

With each passing day, I found myself drawn to Daniel more deeply, my heart yearning for the chance to know him better. The mere thought of him sent butterflies fluttering in my stomach, a whirlwind of emotions swirling within me like a tempestuous sea.

But with the sweetness of love came the bitter sting of uncertainty, the fear of rejection looming like a shadow over my newfound emotions. Would Daniel feel the same way? Or was our brief encounter nothing more than a fleeting moment in time, destined to fade into memory like a whisper in the wind?

As I grappled with these feelings, I couldn't help but wonder what lay ahead on the winding road of love. Was it worth risking my heart for the chance at something more? Only time would tell, as I navigated the turbulent waters of love's sweet embrace, unsure of what the future held but willing to brave the journey nonetheless.

There was one time I was in the quiet of my room, bathed in the soft glow of lamplight, I found solace in the pages of an old photo album. Each faded image held a fragment of a life I could scarcely remember, faces frozen in time, their stories waiting to be told.

A gentle knock on the door interrupted my reverie, and I looked up to see Agnes standing in the doorway, concern etched on her features.

"Clara, is everything okay?" she asked, her voice filled with genuine concern.

I offered her a weak smile, though the weight of my loneliness still pressed heavily upon me. "I'm fine, Agnes. Just lost in thought, I suppose." Agnes stepped into the room, her presence a comforting balm to my troubled soul. "Mind if I join you?"

I shook my head, grateful for the company. "Not at all. Please, have a seat."

As Agnes settled onto the bed beside me, her warmth enveloped me like a protective shield. "You've been quiet lately," she observed, her eyes filled with empathy. "Is there anything you want to talk about?" I hesitated, unsure of how to put my feelings into words. "It's just... sometimes I feel like there's a part of me that's missing," I confessed, my voice barely above a whisper. "I don't remember who I was before I came here, and it's like... like I'm searching for something I can't quite grasp."

Agnes reached out and took my hand in hers, her touch a gentle reassurance. "I understand, Clara. It's okay to feel lost sometimes. We'll figure it out together, I promise." Her words were like a lifeline in the sea of uncertainty, offering me hope in the midst of my despair. With Agnes by my side, I knew that I didn't have to face my loneliness alone.

The next morning, I found myself once again in the familiar warmth of Agnes's kitchen, the comforting aroma of freshly baked bread filling the air. As I busied myself with arranging pastries on the display, a sudden clumsiness took over me, causing a tray to tip over. A cascade of croissants tumbled to the floor, and I hurriedly bent down to gather them, cheeks flushed with embarrassment.

"Need some help with that?" a warm, familiar voice asked.

I looked up to see Daniel standing there, a friendly smile on his face. His presence instantly brightened the room, and I couldn't help but feel a flutter in my chest.

"Oh, thank you," I replied, trying to regain my composure. "I'm usually not this clumsy, I promise." He laughed softly, his eyes twinkling with amusement. "Don't worry about it. Happens to the best of us."

As he helped me pick up the croissants, our hands brushed briefly, sending a jolt of warmth through me. I glanced up at him, meeting his gaze, and for a moment, the world seemed to stand still. "Daniel," he said, offering his hand once we were both standing again. "We met at the charity event, remember?"

"Yes, I remember," I replied, shaking his hand and feeling a strange sense of familiarity and comfort in his presence. "I am just stopping by to see if you and Agnes needed any help with the upcoming event this weekend. I figured I could lend a hand."

Agnes, who had been watching our interaction with a knowing smile, stepped forward. "We'd love that, Daniel. Thank you for offering." Over the course of the day, Daniel's presence became a constant. He helped with deliveries, assisted customers, and even tried his hand at baking, much to the amusement of Agnes and myself. We spent hours talking, sharing stories, and laughing together, and with each passing moment, I felt our connection deepen. One afternoon, as we were finishing up the day's work, Daniel turned to me with a curious expression. "Clara, can I ask you something?"

"Sure," I replied, intrigued by the serious tone in his voice. "Have you ever felt like you're carrying around a secret, even if you can't quite name it?" I paused, taken aback by his perceptiveness. "What do you mean?"

"It's like there's this depth to you, something unspoken," he said, searching for the right words. "It's in your eyes, like you have a story that's waiting to be told." His words struck a chord deep within me, and for a moment, I was at a loss for how to respond. "I guess you could say I'm still piecing my story together," I said softly, avoiding his gaze. "There are parts of my past that are a bit hazy."

Daniel nodded thoughtfully, his expression gentle. "Whenever you're ready to share, I'm here to listen." His kindness and understanding touched me deeply, and I felt a surge of gratitude for his presence in my life. "Thank you, Daniel. That means a lot."

As the day turned into evening, I found myself looking forward to every moment spent with Daniel. His warmth and sincerity made me feel seen and understood in a way I had never experienced before. Yet, amidst the blossoming connection, I also grappled with the growing emotions that stirred within me. One evening, as we walked together through the quiet streets of Meadowbrook, the sky painted with the hues of the setting sun, I found myself on the verge of confessing my feelings.

"Daniel, there's something I need to tell you," I began, my heart pounding in my chest.

He stopped and turned to face me, his expression attentive and curious. "What is it, Clara?" But as the words formed on my lips, a wave of uncertainty washed over me. What if he didn't feel the same way? What if our friendship was put at risk?

"It's nothing," I said quickly, forcing a smile. "I just wanted to thank you for everything. You've been a wonderful friend."

Daniel's eyes softened, and he reached out to gently squeeze my hand. "You're welcome, Clara. I'm glad to have you in my life." As we continued our walk, the unspoken emotions hung heavy in the air between us. And though I didn't have the courage to voice my feelings just yet, I knew that our connection was something special, something worth holding onto.

After my encounter with Daniel, I returned to the bakery with a mix of excitement and confusion. Agnes was busy arranging freshly baked loaves on the shelves, but she looked up with a warm smile as I entered. "Clara, you're back," she greeted. "And you look like you've got something on your mind." I tried to hide my swirling emotions, but Agnes's knowing gaze seemed to see right through me.

"Come on, let's sit down," she said, leading me to a small table in the corner. The comforting aroma of baked goods filled the air, and I felt a sense of calm wash over me.

"It's about Daniel," I began, unsure of how to articulate my feelings. "I can't stop thinking about him, and I don't understand why." Agnes gave me a knowing look. "Ah, I see. You might have a crush on him."

"A crush?" I repeated, the word sounding foreign on my tongue. "What does that even mean?" Agnes chuckled softly. "It's when you feel a strong attraction to someone, often accompanied by a desire to spend more time with them and get to know them better."

I pondered her words, trying to make sense of my emotions. "But why do I feel this way? Why does thinking about him make my heart race and my stomach flutter?"

"That's the mystery of love," Agnes said gently. "It's an emotion that can be both exhilarating and terrifying. It makes us feel alive in ways we never imagined."

I sighed, feeling more confused than ever. "How do you know if it's real? If it's not just a fleeting feeling?"

Agnes reached across the table and took my hand in hers. "Clara, love is a journey. It's not always clear or straightforward, but it's worth exploring. Give yourself time to understand your feelings. Let things unfold naturally." Her words brought a sense of comfort, but also a new wave of questions. "What if he doesn't feel the same way? What if I'm just imagining everything?"

"That's a risk we all take," Agnes said with a reassuring smile. "But you'll never know unless you give it a chance. Trust your heart, Clara. It knows the way." I nodded, feeling a mixture of hope and uncertainty. "Thank you, Agnes. You've given me a lot to think about." "Anytime, dear," she said warmly. "Now, why don't you help me with these pastries? It'll take your mind off things for a while."

I joined Agnes behind the counter, grateful for the distraction. Even with Agnes's comforting words and support, a nagging sense of loneliness lingered in the back of my mind. As I lay in bed that night, the darkness of the room seemed to amplify the echoes of my thoughts. Who was I, truly? The more I tried to remember, the more elusive my past seemed to become.

Chapter 5
The Weight of Loneliness

The next morning, as the first light of dawn filtered through the curtains, I got up with a heavy heart. It was my fourth day staying with Agnes, and despite the warmth and kindness she had shown me, I still felt like a stranger to myself. I went downstairs to find Agnes already in the kitchen, humming softly as she prepared breakfast.

"Good morning, Clara," she greeted me with a warm smile. "Did you sleep well?"

I forced a smile in return. "I did, thank you." But my voice lacked conviction.

Agnes's eyes softened with concern. "Is everything okay? You seem a bit down this morning."

I took a deep breath, feeling the weight of my unspoken worries. "It's just... sometimes I feel so alone, even when I'm surrounded by people. It's like there's a part of me that's missing." Agnes set down the spatula she was holding and walked over to me. "Clara, you're not alone. You have me, and the people of Meadowbrook who care about you. But I understand that feeling. Sometimes, when we're searching for something, it can make us feel isolated."

I nodded, appreciating her understanding. "Thank you, Agnes. I just wish I could remember more about who I was before I came here." "Give it time," she said gently. "Sometimes, the answers we're looking for come to us when we least expect them."

I smiled faintly, grateful for her reassurance. "You're right. I just need to be patient."

Agnes returned to her cooking, and I joined her in the kitchen, helping her prepare the morning's pastries. As we worked, the scent of freshly baked bread and the warmth of the kitchen helped to soothe my restless mind. Later that day, Agnes suggested we take a walk to clear our heads. As we strolled through the town, I couldn't help but think about Daniel and the connection I felt with him. The memory of our brief conversation at the charity event replayed in my mind.

As if summoned by my thoughts, we rounded a corner and there he was, standing by a flower stall, talking to the vendor. My heart skipped a beat. "Clara, isn't that Daniel?" Agnes whispered, a teasing smile playing on her lips. I nodded, my cheeks flushing. "Yes, it is." Agnes nudged me gently. "Go say hello. You never know where a simple greeting might lead."

Taking a deep breath, I approached Daniel. He turned and saw me, his face lighting up with a warm smile. "Clara, it's good to see you again," he said, his eyes meeting mine.

"Hi, Daniel," I replied, trying to keep my voice steady. "How have you been?"

"I'm good, thanks. Just picking up some flowers for my mother," he said, gesturing to the colorful bouquet in his hand. "What about you? How's everything going?"

I glanced back at Agnes, who gave me an encouraging nod. "I'm doing well. Agnes and I were just out for a walk."

"That's great," Daniel said, his smile widening. "Hey, would you like to join me for a coffee? There's a nice little café just around the corner." My heart fluttered at the invitation. "Sure, I'd love to." As we walked to the café, I couldn't help but feel a sense of excitement and nervousness. Sitting down with Daniel felt like the beginning of something new and wonderful.

The café was cozy, with soft music playing in the background and the rich aroma of coffee filling the air. Daniel and I found a table by the window, and he ordered us both drinks. "So, tell me more about yourself, Clara," he said, his eyes full of curiosity.

I hesitated, not knowing what to say. "There's not much to tell, really. I'm still figuring things out."

Daniel nodded, his expression understanding. "I get that. Life can be pretty confusing sometimes." "What about you?" I asked, eager to shift the focus. "What do you do?"

"I'm a teacher," he said with a smile. "I work at the local school, teaching science to middle school students."

"That sounds amazing," I said, genuinely impressed. "You must have a lot of patience."

Daniel chuckled. "It has its challenges, but I love it. Seeing the kids' faces light up when they understand something new makes it all worth it." As we talked, I felt the connection between us grow stronger. His kindness and warmth were like a balm to my lonely heart, and for the first time in a long while, I felt a glimmer of hope.

The conversation flowed easily, and by the time we finished our drinks, I felt like I had known Daniel for much longer than just a brief encounter at a charity event.

As we left the café, Daniel turned to me. "I had a great time today, Clara. I hope we can do this again soon." "I'd like that," I replied, feeling a genuine smile spread across my face.

We said our goodbyes, and as I walked back to the bakery with Agnes, I felt a sense of lightness in my heart. The weight of loneliness still lingered, but it was tempered by the warmth of new connections and the promise of more to come. That evening, as the sun set and the town was bathed in a golden glow, I reflected on the day's events. The conversations, the laughter, the new connections—all of it filled me with a sense of purpose and belonging. Agnes was at the counter, smiling and chatting with a regular, when her face suddenly went pale. Her hands began to tremble, and before I could react, she crumpled to the floor.

"Agnes!" I cried out, rushing to her side. The bakery fell silent, all eyes on us. "Someone call an ambulance!" A kind-looking woman in the crowd pulled out her phone and dialed emergency services while I tried to keep Agnes conscious. "Stay with me, Agnes. Help is on the way." Her eyes fluttered open for a moment, filled with pain and confusion. "Clara..." she whispered, her voice barely audible.

The ambulance arrived quickly, and the paramedics worked efficiently to stabilize Agnes and get her onto a stretcher. I followed them to the local Hospital, my heart pounding with fear and worry. The ride felt like an eternity, every second stretching into an agonizing wait. At the Hospital, they rushed Agnes into the emergency room, leaving me in the waiting area, filled with anxiety. I paced back and forth, the sterile smell of the Hospital doing nothing to calm my nerves. The minutes ticked by, each one heavier than the last.

As I waited, the door swung open and Daniel walked in, his face etched with concern. "Clara, I heard what happened. Is she alright?" "I don't know," I replied, my voice shaky. "She just collapsed out of nowhere. They're with her now."

Daniel placed a reassuring hand on my shoulder. "She's strong, Clara. She'll pull through this." We sat together in the waiting room, Daniel's presence providing a small measure of comfort amidst the chaos of my thoughts. Finally, after what felt like an eternity, a doctor emerged from the emergency room.

"Miss Clara?" he called. I jumped to my feet. "Yes, that's me. How is she?"

The doctor's expression was grave. "Agnes has had a collapse due to complications from her cancer." Daniel's hand remained a comforting presence on my shoulder, anchoring me amidst the storm of my thoughts. "What do we do now?" I asked, my voice barely above a whisper.

The doctor's gaze softened with sympathy as she shook her head. "I'm sorry, Miss Clara. Agnes is still unconscious, but we are doing everything they can to stabilize her. It's going to be a long night." Despair washed over me like a tidal wave, threatening to pull me under. But as I turned to Daniel, his unwavering support was a beacon of light in the darkness. "We'll stay by her side," he said softly, his voice filled with determination. "She won't be alone."

Relief washed over me, but I knew the worry wasn't entirely gone. As Agnes rested, Daniel and I sat in the small clinic café, trying to process everything. "Clara," Daniel began gently, "you looked terrified when Agnes collapsed. She's really important to you, isn't she?" "She is," I admitted, my voice barely above a whisper. "She's been like a guiding light since I arrived in Meadowbrook. I can't imagine this place without her."

Daniel nodded, understanding in his eyes. "It's hard when someone we care about is hurting. But she's in good hands now. And you're not alone. I'm here for you."

I looked down at my hands, feeling the weight of his words. "I just wish I could do more." "Being here, caring for her, that's already more than enough," he said softly. "Sometimes, just being there for someone can make all the difference."

The night wore on, each passing hour weighed down by the heavy burden of worry. Agnes lay still in her hospital bed, her breathing shallow and labored, a stark reminder of the fragility of life. Daniel and I sat in vigil by her side, our silent presence a testament to the bond we shared with our dear friend. The hospital corridors were hushed, the only sound the soft hum of machinery and the occasional footsteps of passing nurses.

As the hours stretched on, fatigue began to take its toll, both physically and emotionally. My eyes grew heavy with exhaustion, but I dared not close them, fearful of what I might miss in those fleeting moments of rest. Daniel sensed my weariness and offered a small smile of encouragement. "You should get some rest, Clara," he said softly. "I'll stay here with Agnes." But I shook my head, unable to tear myself away from her side. "I can't leave her," I replied, my voice tinged with a hint of desperation.

Daniel reached out and gently squeezed my hand. "She wouldn't want you to exhaust yourself like this," he insisted. "We need you to be strong for her." His words struck a chord deep within me, reminding me of the importance of self-care in times of crisis. With a reluctant nod, I conceded, allowing Daniel to guide me to a nearby waiting area where I could rest. As I settled into an uncomfortable chair, sleep eluded me, my thoughts consumed by worry for Agnes. The minutes dragged on like hours, each one filled with a sense of restless anticipation.

Finally, as the first light of dawn began to filter through the windows, a nurse approached with an update on Agnes's condition. My heart leaped with hope as she delivered the news—Agnes was stable, her condition improving with each passing hour. Relief washed over me like a wave, buoying my spirits and filling me with renewed determination. With a grateful smile, I rose from my seat, ready to return to Agnes's side and continue our vigil together.

As the morning light filtered through the curtains, casting a warm glow over the room, I found myself drawn to Agnes's bedside, a silent prayer forming on my lips. With trembling hands, I reached out to clasp hers, the connection grounding me amidst the uncertainty that hung in the air. "Agnes," I whispered, my voice barely above a murmur. "If you can hear me, please know that you're not alone. We're all here with you, holding you in our hearts and thoughts."

Tears pricked at the corners of my eyes as I continued, the weight of my words heavy with emotion. "You've always been the heart and soul of our little community, Agnes. Your kindness, your generosity—they've touched so many lives, including mine." Hours passed in quiet contemplation, each moment stretching into an eternity as we waited for any sign of improvement. And then, as if in response to our unspoken prayers, Agnes stirred, her eyelids fluttering open for the first time since her collapse.

A wave of relief washed over me, tears of gratitude streaming down my cheeks as I reached out to grasp her hand. "Agnes," I whispered, my voice choked with emotion. "You're awake."

Agnes's gaze met mine, her eyes filled with a mixture of confusion and recognition. "Clara? Daniel?" she murmured, her voice weak but filled with relief. "What... what happened?" As Daniel and I exchanged a knowing glance, a sense of hope bloomed within me. Agnes struggled to piece together the events that had led to her collapse, Daniel stepped forward, his voice gentle but filled with concern. "You had a bit of a scare, Agnes," he explained, his eyes reflecting the relief that washed over him at her awakening. "But you're safe now. We're here with you."

Agnes blinked, her gaze drifting from Daniel to me and back again as if trying to make sense of the situation. "I... I remember feeling dizzy," she murmured, her brow furrowing in concentration. "And then everything went black." I nodded, offering her a reassuring smile. "You had a collapse, Agnes," I said softly. "But the doctors are taking care of you now. You're going to be okay."

A flicker of uncertainty crossed Agnes's features, her eyes clouded with worry. "What about the bakery?" she asked, her voice tinged with concern. "I don't want to let anyone down." Daniel reached out and gently squeezed her hand, his touch a source of comfort amidst the turmoil of her thoughts. "Don't worry about that, Agnes," he reassured her.

"Right now, the most important thing is your health. The bakery can wait." Agnes nodded, a faint smile gracing her lips as she squeezed our hands in return. "Thank you," she whispered, her voice filled with gratitude. "For being here. For everything."

Tears welled up in my eyes as I leaned in to embrace her, the weight of the moment lifting from my shoulders as we held each other in a tight embrace.

Chapter 6
The Revelation

I felt the weight of our shared journey lift from my shoulders, replaced by a deep-seated determination to stand by Agnes's side no matter what challenges lay ahead. In that moment of solidarity, surrounded by the warmth of friendship and love, I knew that together, we could weather any storm.

With a final squeeze of Agnes's hand, I stepped back, my eyes meeting Daniel's with a silent understanding. We may not have all the answers, but as long as we faced the future together, there was nothing we couldn't overcome.

As the evening stretched on, we remained by Agnes's side, offering words of encouragement and silent prayers for her recovery. And though the road ahead was uncertain, I took comfort in the knowledge that we would face it together, bound by the unbreakable bonds of friendship and love.

While Agnes is sleeping, a hushed anticipation filled the hospital room, each passing moment weighted with the uncertainty of Agnes's condition. It was in this solemn atmosphere that a doctor approached me, his expression grave as he delivered news that sent shockwaves through my already fragile heart.

"Clara," the doctor began, his voice gentle but tinged with urgency. "I'm afraid I have difficult news. Agnes's condition has deteriorated rapidly. She suffers from advanced heart failure, exacerbated by a rare form of cancer known as cardiac sarcoma."

My breath caught in my throat, the gravity of the situation crashing down on me like a tidal wave. Agnes, my dear friend, was in desperate need of a heart donor, and time was running out.

"We're doing everything we can to find a match," the doctor continued, his tone solemn. "But the reality is, we need to act fast if we're going to save her."

Numb with shock, I nodded silently, my mind racing as I grappled with the enormity of the task at hand. Agnes's life hung in the balance, and it was up to us to find a donor who could give her the gift of life.

As the doctor left the room, leaving me to wrestle with the weight of his words, a glimmer of hope sparked within me. "Doctor," I called after him. "I have a healthy heart. Can I be a donor?"

The doctor paused, his eyes widening slightly in surprise before a hopeful expression crossed his face. "Yes, Clara, you can," he affirmed, his voice filled with a newfound sense of optimism. "Your heart is healthy and could be a match for Agnes. We'll need to conduct some tests to confirm, but this could be the breakthrough we've been hoping for."

Relief flooded through me at his words, a surge of purpose driving me forward. With a renewed determination, I pledged to do whatever it took to save Agnes's life. Time was of the essence, and every moment counted in our race against the clock.

As I prepared for the tests, my mind raced with a whirlwind of emotions. The prospect of donating my heart was daunting, but the thought of saving Agnes's life filled me with a profound sense of purpose. She had been there for me in my darkest moments, offering unwavering support and friendship, and now it was my turn to repay the favor.

With a deep breath and a silent prayer, I braced myself for the journey ahead, knowing that the road would be fraught with challenges but determined to see it through to the end. Agnes's life hung in the balance, and I would stop at nothing to give her the fighting chance she deserved.

Agnes regained consciousness, I watched the doctor approach her bedside, his expression serious yet hopeful. "Agnes, there's something important I need to discuss with you," he began, his voice steady as he prepared to deliver the news. "We've been searching for a heart donor, and it appears we may have found a potential match."

Agnes's eyes widened with surprise, and I felt a lump form in my throat as I awaited the doctor's revelation. "That's wonderful news," Agnes murmured, her voice filled with cautious hope. "Who's the donor?"

The doctor's gaze shifted towards me before returning to Agnes, and I held my breath, waiting for him to speak. "It's Clara," he revealed, his words hanging heavy in the air. "She's compatible, and her heart could be a match for you."

Agnes's reaction was immediate, her eyes narrowing with anger. "Clara?" she repeated, her voice trembling with emotion. "How dare she even consider such a thing? She's just a child. She has her whole life ahead of her."

I felt a pang of guilt and uncertainty as Agnes's words pierced through me like a knife. Was I being selfish to offer up my own life to save hers? Did I even have the right to make such a monumental decision?

Agnes's anger was palpable as she turned to me, her voice filled with frustration. "Clara, how could you even think of doing this?" she demanded, her eyes burning with intensity. "You're young, you have your whole life ahead of you. You shouldn't have to sacrifice yourself for me."

Tears welled up in my eyes as I struggled to find the right words to respond. "I-I just want to help you, Agnes," I stammered, my voice trembling with emotion. "You've done so much for me, and I can't bear the thought of losing you."

Sensing the tension in the room, the doctor excused himself, leaving Agnes and me alone to grapple with the weight of our emotions. Agnes's expression softened, her anger giving way to sadness and resignation. "I appreciate your gesture, Clara," she said softly, her voice tinged with sorrow. "But I can't let you do this. You deserve to live your life to the fullest, just like anyone else."

As we sat together in the quiet of the hospital room, the weight of our shared emotions hung heavy in the air. In that moment, I knew that our bond was stronger than any medical diagnosis or potential treatment

As Agnes's anger subsided, her expression softened, but her resolve remained firm. "Clara," she said gently, her voice tinged with sadness, "I know you want to help me, but you need to accept that this isn't the answer. You have your whole life ahead of you. You shouldn't have to sacrifice it for me."

Her words cut through me like a knife, and I felt a surge of frustration and helplessness welling up inside me. "But I can't just stand by and do nothing," I protested, my voice trembling with emotion. "You mean everything to me, Agnes. I can't bear to lose you."

Agnes reached out and took my hand, her touch warm and comforting. "I know, Clara," she said softly, her voice filled with compassion. "And I appreciate your love and concern more than you'll ever know. But sometimes, we have to accept things as they are and make the most of the time we have."

Tears welled up in my eyes as I struggled to come to terms with Agnes's words. Deep down, I knew she was right, but accepting the reality of the situation felt like an impossible task. Still, as I looked into her eyes, filled with courage and determination.

Agnes sighed wearily, her eyes flickering with exhaustion. "Clara," she said softly, "I appreciate your concern, I really do. But right now, I just need to rest. I don't want to think about this anymore."

Her words struck me like a blow, the weight of her exhaustion evident in her voice. I nodded silently, swallowing back the lump forming in my throat. "Of course, Agnes," I replied, trying to keep my voice steady. "I'll be here if you need anything."

With a weary smile, Agnes squeezed my hand before closing her eyes, sinking into the pillows as if seeking refuge from the turmoil of her thoughts. As I watched her drift off to sleep, a sense of helplessness washed over me, mingled with a fierce determination to do whatever it took to ease her suffering.

And so, as the soft hum of the hospital filled the room, I sat vigil by Agnes's side, silently vowing to support her in whatever way she needed, for as long as she needed me.

As I sat in the dimly lit hospital room, my mind adrift in a sea of uncertainty, I suddenly felt a strange sensation wash over me. It was as if a gentle breeze had whispered through the room, stirring the dormant depths of my consciousness.

At first, it was nothing more than a fleeting whisper, a faint echo of memories long forgotten. But as I closed my eyes and allowed myself to surrender to the sensation, the whispers grew louder, more insistent, until they became a symphony of memories playing out before my mind's eye.

I saw myself bathed in celestial light, my wings unfurled as I soared through the boundless expanse of the heavens. I felt the warmth of divine energy coursing through my veins, filling me with a sense of purpose and belonging that transcended mortal understanding. , I was overcome with a profound sense of clarity. I remembered now—this was not a twist of fate, but a choice I had made. I had volunteered to descend to Earth, to walk among mortals and experience life as they did.

The purpose behind my request echoed in the recesses of my mind—a desire to understand the intricacies of human existence, to witness their joys and sorrows firsthand, and to offer guidance and protection where needed. It was a noble mission, one that I had undertaken willingly, knowing the challenges and sacrifices it would entail. The truth of my identity hit me like a bolt of lightning, electrifying every fiber of my being with its undeniable presence. How had I forgotten who I truly was?

I wasn't just Clara, a mere mortal bound by the limitations of human existence. I was Celestia, an angelic being tasked with a sacred duty to watch over and protect the inhabitants of Earth.

The memories of my celestial existence flooded back, so too did the solemn recollection of the rules that governed my time on Earth. I remembered the sacred decree handed down by the council of angels—that my stay among mortals would be temporary, lasting only seven days.

With a heavy heart, I realized that this was now my fifth day on Earth, leaving me with just two fleeting days remaining before I would return to the heavens. The weight of this realization bore down on me, filling me with a profound sense of sadness and regret.

How could I have forgotten the limitations of my time here? How could I have allowed myself to become so entangled in the affairs of mortals, knowing that my presence among them was but a fleeting whisper in the grand tapestry of eternity?

The gravity of my situation sank in as I grappled with the inevitability of my departure. There were still so many unanswered questions, so many lives left untouched by my presence. And now, with just two days left, I feared that my time on Earth would slip away like grains of sand through an hourglass, leaving me with nothing but memories and regrets.

As the realization dawned upon me, a chill swept through my soul. How could I have been so foolish? In my eagerness to experience the human condition, I had overlooked one of the most fundamental rules of my celestial existence—I was not permitted to fall in love, With a heavy heart, I grappled with the implications of my forbidden feelings. How could I face the inevitable separation from Daniel, knowing that our connection was fated to be fleeting and transient? How could I reconcile the longing in my heart with the knowledge that it was forbidden by the very laws that governed my existence?

But even in the face of such overwhelming sadness, I knew that I could not afford to dwell on what could have been. Instead, I resolved to make the most of the time I had left, to cherish each moment as if it were my last, and to leave behind a legacy of love and compassion that would endure long after I had returned to the heavens.

The weight of my impending departure bearing down on me, I knew that time was of the essence. Despite the forbidden nature of my feelings, I couldn't ignore the deep bond that had formed between Agnes and me during my brief time on Earth. If I couldn't have the love I desired, then perhaps I could find solace in the act of selfless sacrifice.

Determined to make the most of the time I had left, I resolved to do everything in my power to help Agnes, to offer her the chance of a future that had been denied to her by the cruel hand of fate. Despite the risks and uncertainties that lay ahead, I knew that I couldn't turn away from her plight, not when her life hung in the balance.

Determined to give Agnes the fighting chance she deserved, I made a secret appointment with the doctor, concealing my intentions from Agnes and the rest of the world. With a heavy heart and a sense of urgency driving me forward, I outlined my plan for a heart transplant, knowing that it was the only chance Agnes had for survival.

Despite the risks and uncertainties that lay ahead, I couldn't shake the feeling that this was the right course of action. I was willing to risk everything, even my own safety and happiness, to give Agnes a chance at a future free from the shadow of illness and despair.

As I awaited the appointment, a sense of unease gnawed at the edges of my consciousness. I knew that I was treading dangerous territory, playing with forces beyond my control. But in the end, the thought of losing Agnes was a risk I couldn't afford to take. And so, with determination burning in my heart, I forged ahead, praying that my actions would not come at too great a cost.

Chapter 7
The Weight of Forbidden Love

As the weight of my decision bore down upon me, Outside the room there is a long chair where Daniel and I sit at some point I knew that I had to share the truth with Daniel, No matter how difficult it may be. With a heavy heart and trembling hands, I sought him out in the quiet sanctuary of the evening, knowing that our conversation would forever alter the course of our lives.

"Daniel," I began, my voice barely a whisper in the stillness of the night. "There's something I need to tell you." He turned to face me, his eyes searching mine for answers. "What is it, Clara? You seem... troubled."

Taking a deep breath, I gathered my courage, knowing that there was no turning back now. "I've made a decision," I confessed, my voice trembling with emotion. "I'm going to donate my heart to Agnes." A stunned silence fell over us, the weight of my words hanging in the air like a heavy fog. I watched as Daniel's expression shifted from confusion to shock, his eyes widening in disbelief.

"You're what?" he exclaimed, his voice filled with incredulity. "But... but why? Why would you do such a thing?" Tears welled up in my eyes as I struggled to find the words to explain the depth of my feelings. "Agnes is dying, Daniel," I explained, my voice trembling with emotion. "She needs a heart transplant to survive, and I'm a match. I couldn't just stand by and do nothing while she suffers."

In a moment of vulnerability, I laid bare my heart to Daniel, the words spilling forth with a mixture of longing and regret. "Daniel," I began, my voice steady despite the tumult of emotions swirling within me.

"I wish we had more time together. More moments to share, more memories to make." Daniel's eyes softened with understanding as he listened, his gaze meeting mine with a depth of feeling that mirrored my own. "Clara," he replied softly, his voice tinged with a hint of sadness. "I feel the same way. If only things were different, if only we had met sooner." A pang of longing gripped my heart as I reached out to him, my hand seeking solace in his touch. "Me too," I admitted, a wistful smile tugging at the corners of my lips. "But I'm grateful for the time we've had, however brief it may be."

As we stood there, enveloped in the quiet intimacy of our shared confession, I felt a sense of peace wash over me. Despite the uncertainty of our future, I took solace in the depth of our connection, in the knowledge that our love would endure, transcending the constraints of time and circumstance. As I poured out my heart to Daniel, his expression shifted from surprise to confusion, then finally to a profound sense of concern. His brows furrowed as he struggled to comprehend the depth of my resolve, his eyes searching mine for answers that I could scarcely provide.

"Clara," he began, his voice laced with uncertainty. "I don't understand. Why do you seem so... resigned to this? Why do you seem to know or want to go?"

I hesitated, grappling with the weight of his questions and the truth that lay buried within my heart. How could I explain to him the inexplicable pull that tugged at my soul, the whispered promises of destiny that beckoned me homeward?

"It's hard to explain," I replied, my voice barely above a whisper. "But I just... know. Deep down, I know that this is where I'm meant to be. This is where I belong."

Daniel's brow furrowed further, his confusion giving way to a growing sense of frustration. "But why?" he pressed, his voice tinged with desperation. "Why do you have to leave? Why can't you stay here with us?" I struggled to find the words to convey the truth that lay heavy upon my heart. "Because I'm not like you, Daniel," I whispered, the words tasting bitter on my tongue. "I'm not meant for this world. I'm meant to return to where I belong, to the heavens above."

Then, in Daniel's eyes, I saw a spark of incredulity mingled with a flicker of anger. "How?" he demanded, his voice edged with disbelief. "How do you know? You're not a god, Clara. You can't predict the future." A heavy silence settled between us as I struggled to articulate the inexplicable knowledge that had settled in the depths of my being. "I can't explain it," I admitted, my voice trembling with uncertainty. "But I feel it, Daniel. Deep within my soul, I feel the pull of destiny guiding me home."

Daniel's frustration turned to resignation, his gaze softened, and he reached out to gently cradle my face in his hands. "Clara," he murmured, his voice tinged with sorrow. "I may not understand why you feel this way, but I can't deny the depth of your conviction. If this is truly your path, then I can only wish that we had met sooner."

Tears welled up in my eyes at his words, a bittersweet ache settling in my chest. "I wish the same," I whispered, leaning into his touch. "But even though I must leave, know that I'll be watching over you both from above. I'll always be with you, in spirit if not in flesh."

Daniel's eyes shimmered with unshed tears as he nodded, a mixture of emotions evident in his gaze. "Clara," he said softly, his voice thick with emotion. "I don't know how to thank you for what you're doing. It's more than anyone should ever ask of another." A melancholy smile graced my lips as I returned his gaze. "You don't need to thank me," I replied, my voice filled with quiet resolve. "I'm simply doing what I must. For Agnes. For someone I hold dear."

With a final, lingering embrace, we parted ways, each lost in our own thoughts and emotions. As I made my way towards my fate, I couldn't help but wonder at the depths of love and sacrifice that bound us together, even in the face of the unknown. Then the doctor entered the room, I felt a jolt of anticipation and apprehension course through me so I decided to follow her as well

. Agnes lay on the hospital bed, her eyes hopeful yet clouded with uncertainty.

"Miss Agnes," the doctor began, his tone serious yet compassionate. "We have some promising news. A heart donor has come forward, willing to undergo the transplant procedure. If you're willing, we can proceed with the surgery as soon as tomorrow."

Agnes's eyes widened with a mix of surprise and relief. "Oh, thank goodness," she murmured, her voice filled with gratitude.

My heart sank at his words, a pang of confusion and disbelief coursing through me. I hadn't scheduled any donation yet, so who could it be? As I struggled to comprehend the unexpected turn of events, Agnes's face lit up with hope, oblivious to the turmoil raging within me. The doctor's words echoed in my head – a heart donor had been found. Relief bloomed on Agnes' face, chasing away the worry lines etched there. My own heart, however, did a surprised flip-flop. I hadn't even signed the donation papers yet, we'd only talked about it as a last resort. Who on earth could this mystery donor be?

A million questions swirled in my head, but Agnes' grateful smile stole my voice. "Oh, Clara," she breathed, her voice weak but filled with hope. "You don't have to do this anymore. Someone wonderful has come forward." My mind reeled. I was supposed to be the donor. We'd discussed it, the fear a constant shadow in both our hearts. But now, someone else had stepped up, leaving me utterly confused. "Agnes, wait," I stammered, the words tumbling out before I could stop them. "I never..."

She squeezed my hand, her touch frail but reassuring. "There's no need to explain, dear. This is a miracle. We don't need to understand, just be grateful." Grateful? Relief should have flooded me, but instead, a strange emptiness settled in my chest. Was I relieved I wouldn't have to make such a huge sacrifice? Or was there a part of me, a hidden well of selflessness, that actually wanted to give Agnes this chance, this new lease on life?

The silence stretched on, pregnant with unspoken questions and a tangle of emotions I couldn't quite decipher. "Who is it?" I asked finally, my voice barely a whisper.

Agnes shook her head, a flicker of confusion crossing her face. "The doctor wouldn't say. He said they wanted to remain anonymous." Anonymous. The same word the doctor used for me. But it couldn't be a coincidence, could it? This faceless donor, this mystery savior, had stolen my moment, my chance to save Agnes. Or had they, in a strange twist of fate, set me free?

The news hung heavy in the air. Agnes slept peacefully, the rhythmic beep of the heart monitor a counterpoint to the storm brewing within me. Relief should have been a tidal wave, washing away the fear that had clung to me for weeks. A stranger, an anonymous angel, had stepped forward, offering Agnes a second chance. Yet, a strange emptiness gnawed at me. I hadn't volunteered. We hadn't even finalized the paperwork. Agnes and I had discussed it, a desperate option whispered in hushed tones. Now, that option was gone. Replaced by a mystery donor, a faceless savior who had stolen my moment, my chance to save my friend.

Curiosity, laced with a bitter edge, propelled me towards the nurses' station. The sterile white walls felt like a cruel joke, offering no solace for the turmoil within. A young nurse with kind eyes looked up from her chart. "Excuse me," I began, my voice barely a whisper. "Do you know anything about the heart donor? The doctor said they wanted to remain anonymous, but..."

The nurse shook her head, a sympathetic frown creasing her brow. "Honestly, Clara, I don't. Donors often choose anonymity. Patient confidentiality is paramount."

Disappointment, cold and heavy, settled in my gut. No clues, no whispers, no way to understand this sudden turn of events. Agnes and I had prepared for the worst, for the agonizing sacrifice I might have to make. Now, that path was closed, leaving me adrift.

"There must be something," I pleaded, the words catching in my throat. "A name, a message, anything?" The nurse offered a gentle smile, but her eyes held a flicker of helplessness. "Honey, sometimes these things just happen. A stranger hears a story, feels a connection, and decides to act. It's a beautiful thing, really."

A beautiful thing, she said. But it felt like a theft, a stolen opportunity to prove my love, my loyalty. Relief battled with a strange sense of loss, a hollowness that echoed with the unanswered question: who? Back in Agnes's room, the rhythmic beep of the monitor mocked me. It was a lifeline, a testament to someone else's selfless act, but it wasn't mine. Agnes slept on, oblivious to the storm raging within me.

Sleep eluded me that night. Memories flickered like a dying flame – Agnes, pale and weak, her hand clutching mine with a desperate strength. Our whispered promises, the fear a constant companion. Now, the weight of that fear lifted, replaced by a different kind of burden – the burden of not knowing, of not being the one to save her.

As dawn painted the sky with streaks of pink and orange, a cold truth settled in my stomach. There was no other solution. I couldn't change the past, couldn't pry open the veil of anonymity. All I could do was be there for Agnes, a constant presence as she navigated this new chapter, a chapter gifted by a stranger.

Chapter 8
Truly that's Love

The sterile white walls of the waiting room blurred as exhaustion gnawed at me. Sleep was a distant luxury. Scenes replayed in my mind, each frame a reminder of the impossible situation I found myself in. There was Daniel, the man I'd confessed my feelings to yesterday, standing confidently beside a doctor. It was the same doctor who would operate on Agnes. A familiar pang settled in my chest, a sensation that mimicked human sadness. I, an angel, had descended to the mortal realm to understand human emotions. Now, I was faced with a yearning I couldn't act upon. Angels weren't supposed to fall in love, especially not with the fleeting lives of humans. We were observers, chroniclers, not participants in the grand human drama.

Just then, Daniel stepped in the position I am in . My breath hitched. Here, in the sterile confines of the waiting room, his presence felt strangely comforting, a flicker of warmth amidst the cold anxiety. "Clara," he said, his voice low and concerned. "I heard about Agnes." "Heard?" I echoed, surprise flashing in my eyes. "How?" He hesitated, a flicker of something unreadable crossing his face. "News travels fast in this hospital," he offered finally, a touch too casually. My gaze narrowed. There was something more to it, I was sure. But before I could press him, he cleared his throat.

"She's in surgery, isn't she?" he asked, his voice gentle.

I nodded, the weight of the situation pressing down on me. "They're preparing for operation as we speak." A deep sadness clouded his eyes, a stark contrast to his usual confident demeanor. "I know how much she means to you," he said softly. Gratitude welled up within me. Despite the awkwardness, his presence offered a much-needed anchor in the swirling storm of emotions. We settled into a tense silence, the only sound the rhythmic beeping of the heart monitor echoing in the sterile room. Hours ticked by, each one an eternity. The weight of my impending departure pressed down on me, a bittersweet burden that threatened to steal the joy of Agnes' potential recovery.

Suddenly, Daniel straightened. "I should get going," he said, his voice laced with regret. "I have things to take care of." A pang shot through me. "Already?"

He met my gaze, a flicker of something unreadable passing through his eyes. "I..." he hesitated, then blurted out, "Goodbye, Clara." The word hung in the air, heavy with unspoken emotions. Before I could stop myself, a desperate plea escaped my lips. "We'll meet again, won't we?"

He faltered, surprised by the intensity in my voice. Then, a smile touched his lips, sad but resolute. "In time, we will," he echoed, a promise hanging in the air. With a final lingering look, he turned and disappeared through the door, leaving behind a silence that felt deafening. "In time," I whispered to myself, the words hollow on my tongue. My heart ached with a sense of loss that felt alien and profound. In just a short time, I would be returning to my celestial plane, leaving behind the only human connection I had ever truly felt. Yet, Daniel's words offered a flicker of hope, a faint echo of a future reunion. But for now, all I had was the agonizing wait and the burden of a goodbye that wasn't quite an ending.

Time seemed to stretch and compress all at once. Minutes ticked by like hours, each one an eternity punctuated by the rhythmic beeping of the heart monitor. The fluorescent lights hummed overhead, casting a sterile glow on the waiting room that did little to alleviate the gnawing anxiety in my gut. The goodbye with Daniel echoed in mind. His promise of a future meeting offered a sliver of hope, but it couldn't erase the imminent pain of leaving. Just as despair threatened to consume me, the door swung open, revealing Dr. Thompson.

His face, usually etched with a professional calm, displayed a hint of worry. "Clara," he began, his voice surprisingly gentle. "We're ready for surgery. Agnes is prepped and in good spirits." Relief washed over me, momentarily pushing aside the ache in my chest. Agnes was going to get her second chance. The doctor hesitated for a moment, then held out a small notebook. "There's something else," he said. "A nurse told me to give this to you during the surgery." A notebook? Curiosity flickered within me, a momentary distraction from the impending operation. Before I could ask any questions, the doctor hurried away, leaving me alone with the mysterious notebook.

My fingers brushed against the worn leather cover, sending a shiver down my spine. An inscription on the inside cover caught my eye: "To my guardian angel." A lump formed in my throat. Guardian angel? Who could have left this for me? Just then, a young nurse hurried in, her face flushed with exertion. "Clara?" she panted. "Dr. Thompson just told me you're Agnes' friend. He said to tell you the surgery is underway and everything is going well so far." I offered a grateful smile. "Thank you," I whispered, the notebook clutched tightly in my hand.

The hours that followed were an agonizing blur. Sleep was a distant dream, replaced by a constant vigil by the waiting room door. Every rustle, every hushed conversation sent my heart pounding. Finally, after what felt like an eternity, the door creaked open. Dr. Thompson emerged, a weary but relieved smile etched on his face.

"The surgery was a success," he announced. "Agnes' body is accepting the new heart remarkably well. She's still under observation, but as of now, she's on the road to recovery."

Tears welled up in my eyes, a mixture of relief and exhaustion. Agnes was going to live. She had a second chance, thanks to the selfless act of an anonymous donor.

Dr. Thompson cleared his throat, his gaze flitting towards the notebook I still held tightly. "There's something you should have," he said, extending it towards me. "It was left with instructions to be given to you after the surgery."

My heart skipped a beat. Could it be related to the inscription on the cover? With trembling hands, I accepted the notebook, a strange apprehension battling with a growing curiosity.

The doctor excused himself, leaving me alone with the weight of the unknown. My gaze drifted back to the inscription, then to the blank page facing it. Taking a deep breath, I opened the notebook, my heart pounding in my chest.

The page wasn't entirely blank. A single, small, dried flower was pressed between the pages, a forget-me-not. Tears welled up in my eyes, blurring my vision. It wasn't a written message, but a silent echo of a goodbye, a reminder of the connection I shared with Daniel.

Exhaustion gnawed at me, relentless and cold, mirroring the turmoil within. Agnes' successful surgery brought a wave of relief so vast it threatened to drown me, but it couldn't erase the impending ache of departure. Hours bled into one another, each tick of the clock a stark reminder of my dwindling time. Then, tucked away in the corner of my bag, I remembered the second notebook – the one Dr. Thompson mentioned. Curiosity, tinged with a sliver of apprehension, propelled me to open it. Unlike the first, this one wasn't blank. Filled with photographs, it served as a visual chronicle of my time on Earth.

There was Agnes, beaming with youthful exuberance, in a thousand candid moments. One picture showed us laughing in a cozy cafe, sunlight filtering through the window and painting warm squares on the table. We were surrounded by steaming mugs of coffee, a testament to the afternoon we spent lost in deep conversation. It was the day we hatched the idea for separate endeavors – a charity gala, and a bake sale we have organize with Agnes at her bakery.

Another photo captured us covered in flour, a dusting of white gracing our hair and clothes. We were in Agnes' tiny bakery, a whirlwind of activity as we prepped for the bake sale. The air hung heavy with the sweet aroma of sugar and cinnamon, a scent that now brought a bittersweet pang to my heart.

Tears welled up in my eyes, blurring the images. These weren't just photographs; they were fragments of memories, tangible threads woven into the tapestry of my human experience. A bittersweet ache settled in my chest, a yearning for a life I could never truly have. With trembling fingers, I turned the last page. Tucked into a hidden pocket was a single sheet of paper, folded neatly. My heart hammered against my ribs as I unfolded it. Unlike the first notebook, the inscription here was absent. This felt... different.

Taking a deep breath, I began to read. The elegant script flowed across the page, each word a brushstroke painting a vivid picture. It spoke of stolen glances across crowded cafes, of whispered conversations during flour-dusted baking sessions, moments that held the weight of unspoken emotions. It spoke of a connection that transcended the boundaries of our worlds, a love that bloomed amidst the chaos of separate dreams and stolen hours. The letter was long, filled with a raw honesty that left me breathless. It spoke of a wish to see the sunrise through human eyes, to experience the warmth of a shared laugh, to feel the simple joys of a life I could never have. It spoke of a sacrifice, a heart given freely in the hope of granting another a chance.

A cold dread crept into my limbs as I read further. The writer spoke of a final goodbye, a whisper on the wind, a promise kept at a terrible cost. My breath caught in my throat as the truth slammed into me. This wasn't just a love letter; it was a confession, a final act of love from the one who had given Agnes the gift of life. Tears streamed down my cheeks, blurring the words on the page. The weight of the realization crushed me. Daniel. The kind, quiet boy who volunteered at the hospital, the one whose gaze lingered a moment too long – he was the guardian angel, the anonymous donor.

The ache in my chest intensified, a suffocating blend of grief and gratitude. He was gone, the love story we shared cut tragically short. Yet, in his absence, Agnes lived.

As I finished reading, a single word echoed in the quiet of the room: "Why?" It wasn't a question directed at the writer, but a desperate plea into the void. Why him? Why such a sacrifice?

The answer remained silent, lost in the wind. But in the quiet of the room, I held the weight of his love, a bittersweet burden that mingled with the ache of departure. I closed my eyes, the image of a forget-me-not pressed against my cheek, and whispered a silent goodbye. The goodbye wasn't just for Agnes or this human world; it was for Daniel, the boy who had touched my heart and saved a life, a love story forever etched in the memory of a single, selfless act.

My dearest Clara,

The lights of the gala must be a distant memory now, replaced by the quiet hum of the hospital. But with the silence comes hope – Agnes lives, and a piece of me lives on within her. A bittersweet miracle, wouldn't you say?

Do you remember the night at the charity gala? You, glowing like a fallen star, filling the room with warmth. Me, a shadow in the corner, watching over the festivities. Our eyes met for a moment, a spark leaping across the crowded space. In that single glance, a connection bloomed – a secret language only our hearts understood.

After that night, stolen moments became our treasure. A shy smile across a crowded hallway, hushed conversations filled with dreams and unspoken desires. I longed to feel the world through your eyes, to hear the joy bubbling in your laugh, to experience even a sliver of the life you cherished.

But unlike you, Clara, I had no one waiting for me. No family, no memories of laughter shared over steaming mugs of coffee. As an orphan, I walked alone, my purpose to be a silent guardian for those in need. When I saw Agnes, her life flickering like a candle about to be snuffed out, a choice slammed into me with the force of a tidal wave.

This isn't a goodbye, Clara. It's a promise whispered on the wind. A promise that even though I'm gone, a part of me will always be with you – in the memories we shared, in the smiles you bring to Agnes' face. Somewhere, somehow, our paths may cross again, beyond the veil that separates our worlds.

Live, Clara. Live with the same warmth and kindness you brought to the gala. Let your laughter echo through the years, a symphony for Agnes and the world. And know this: even as I watch over you both from above, a silent guardian angel, the memory of our connection will forever be etched in my soul.

With a love that transcends words,

Your Daniel, forever your guardian angel.

P.S. Funny you should mention looking up angel names! Mine actually is Seraphiel. Guess you can call me your personal guardian angel with a heavenly name, huh? Just smile for Agnes, Clara, that's all I ask.

Chapter 9
An Eternal Impact

The first light of dawn crept through the sterile hospital window, painting the room in soft hues of pink and orange. Agnes lay nestled in the bed, her breathing a gentle rhythm against the quiet hum of the machines monitoring her vitals. Tears welled in my eyes, blurring the lines between Agnes' peaceful face and the dawning realization that my time as Clara was ending. It felt like a cruel joke – the light of a new day pushing me away just as Agnes, finally on the mend, drifted towards sleep.

A warmth, unlike any I'd ever felt before, spread through me, not from the sun but from somewhere deep within. It was a pull, an undeniable urge that resonated in the very core of my being – the pull of returning home, back to the celestial realm I'd left behind for a time. A pang of sadness echoed in my chest, sharp and raw, as I looked at Agnes. Her sleep held the quiet weight of loss, the knowledge of a friend sacrificed, a life saved at a terrible cost. Daniel's selfless act, a gift that granted Agnes a second chance, had left a gaping hole in their bond, a wound that time would have to heal. Yet, amidst the grief etched onto Agnes' face, I saw a flicker of something else – a spark of determination, a resolve to live the life Daniel had so generously bestowed upon her.

With a silent goodbye whispered on the wind, a goodbye only my heart could truly understand, I rose. The familiar pull of the celestial realm grew stronger, a magnetic force guiding me back. As I ascended, a strange sensation washed over me, an ethereal wave that felt like the receding tide of memory. The memories of my time as Clara, so vivid just moments ago, started to fade like mist evaporating under the harsh gaze of the midday sun. The laughter shared with Daniel in the bustling hospital hallway, the stolen glances across the crowded charity gala, the warmth of his hand in mine – all began to blur, the edges softening, the details dissolving into a bittersweet haze.

Yet, a deeper understanding remained, a profound shift within the very fabric of my being. A newfound appreciation for the fragility of human life, the fleeting beauty of their existence, the intensity of their emotions that burned so brightly, even in the face of loss. Seraphiel, the guardian angel, was forever changed by his experience as Daniel. He had walked among humans, felt their joys and sorrows, witnessed the fierce love that bound them together.

Back in the celestial realm, the familiar vastness unfolded before me. I was Celestia again, but I was no longer the same. Within me resided a spark, a flicker of the warmth I felt as Clara. It was a reminder of the love story that bloomed amidst sacrifice, a testament to the enduring connections that could bridge the gap between the celestial and the human. As I gazed upon the endless expanse of the celestial plane, a single tear, imbued with the essence of humanity, traced a path down my cheek. It was a tear for Agnes, for Daniel, and for the bittersweet beauty of human life.

The celestial expanse stretched before me, a dizzying tapestry of swirling stardust and ethereal light. But my gaze remained stubbornly fixed on the distant speck that was Earth. A pang of longing echoed in my chest, a strange sensation for a being who'd existed for millennia.

Memories, once vivid and clear, now danced at the edges of my consciousness – whispers of laughter shared with Daniel, the comforting weight of Agnes' hand in hers. The human experience, though fading like mist at sunrise, had left an indelible mark.

Suddenly, a flicker of movement on Earth caught my eye. It was Agnes, stepping out of the bakery, a bright smile gracing her lips as she greeted a customer. But it wasn't just the smile. There was a newfound strength in her posture, a spark of determination in her eyes. A warmth, different from the celestial kind, bloomed in my chest. It was the bittersweet joy of witnessing the life I helped preserve, the love story that continued even in my absence.

A gentle voice, soft as a summer breeze, echoed in my mind. It was Gabriel, the archangel of communication and hope. His presence, a comforting reminder of home. "Your journey, Celestia," he said, his voice resonating with a celestial melody, "has changed you. You've experienced the profound love and resilience of humanity. This knowledge will forever be a part of you, a bridge between the celestial and the mortal realms."

I turned to face him, a single tear tracing a luminous path down my cheek. "I will never forget them, Gabriel," I whispered. "Never forget the love, the loss, the beauty of being human."

Gabriel smiled, a radiant warmth that filled the celestial plane. "And they, in turn, will carry a piece of you within them," he replied. "A guardian angel touched by their love, forever a testament to the connections that transcend even the boundaries of existence."

As I took my place among the celestial beings once more, I knew I was forever changed. I was Celestia, the guardian angel, but I was also a part of Clara, forever bound to the human experience by the invisible threads of love, loss, and the bittersweet beauty of life.

Acknowledgments

Thishis journey wouldn't have been possible without the love and support of some extraordinary individuals.

First and foremost, my deepest gratitude goes to my friend, **Tricia**. Her unwavering belief in me and my stories fueled me through countless late nights and bouts of self-doubt. Her willingness to listen to every plot twist, character arc, and emotional breakdown was a gift beyond measure. Thank you, Tricia, for being my personal cheerleader and confidante.

To my sister, **Amor**, a heartfelt thank you for being my first reader. Your insightful feedback pushed me to refine the story and explore its depths. Your genuine enthusiasm kept me motivated and eager to share "A Week in Mortal Skin" with the world.

To my entire family, your constant love and encouragement were the wind beneath my wings. Thank you for celebrating every milestone, big and small, and for believing in the power of my dreams. Your unwavering support provided the foundation on which this story was built.

A special thank you to Canva. Their design tools played a crucial role in bringing the cover of this book to life. The platform's accessibility and ease of use allowed me to translate the visual essence of "A Week in Mortal Skin" into a captivating image.

Finally, to my readers, thank you for picking up this book and embarking on this journey with Celestia. I poured my heart and soul into these pages, and I hope you find the story as captivating and thought-provoking as I found the process of writing it.

Author Bio

Viola Giselle crafts fantastical stories where magic dances with the real world. A lifelong devotee of fantasy, Viola draws inspiration from the boundless possibilities of imagination and the enduring strength of the human spirit.

Viola's passion for fantasy translates into captivating narratives that explore themes of love, loss, and transformation. She invites readers to journey alongside her characters, delving into the depths of human emotions and the unbreakable bonds that connect us.

Beyond writing, Viola finds a delightful balance between the fantastical and the delicious. When she's not crafting worlds of magic, she's busy learning the art of pastry, a skill that adds a touch of sweetness to her life (though perhaps not to her waistline!)

www.ingramcontent.com/pod-product-compliance
Lightning Source LLC
Chambersburg PA
CBHW052232150726
48002CB00003B/1394